Lil Mar

"Losing His Balance"

Written by LaMar Sharpe
Illustrated by Grayson Switzer

LUCia

Copyright 2019 LaMar D. Sharpe
lamar@beabetterme.org

ISBN-13: 978-1-7340740-0-0
ISBN-10: 1-7340740-0-0

First Printing October 2019

Dedicated to all those people who change the
lives of others by living as an example and
by empowering others for greatness.

Thank you

LaMar D. Sharpe

Mrs. Adams

Lucia

DJ

Elec

Lil Mar

Lil Mar's Mom

Officer Sharpe

It's Friday 7:30am and it is the last day of school for the week. The sound of an alarm is ringing loudly in the background, 'RING!' 'RING!' 'RING!' 'RING!!!'

A voice softly echoes from behind a slightly open door, "Lil Mar, time to get up and get ready for school son," says Lil Mar's mother.

"Okay, Mom, I'm up and ready to get my day started," he replies. Lil Mar jumps out of bed, and brushes his teeth. Then he puts on his clothes that he had neatly placed out for school the previous night. He heads downstairs to grab his book bag and his breakfast before scattering out of the door.

Before he hurries out of the house to get to his bus stop, he gives his mom a big kiss and hug as he says, "I love you Mom, and thank you for the breakfast."

"I love you, too, Lil Mar. Have a great day at school," says his mom. Then, off he goes to the bus stop.

Lil Mar's bus arrives at his school, Bulldog Leadership Academy, and he begins to walk to his first class. On the way to class, Lil Mar stops and says hello to a few of his friends Elec, DJ, and Lucia.

"Hey, Lil Mar!" says Elec.

"Hi guys!" Lil Mar replies, as he gives all of his friends a high five.

"Lil Mar, do you want to come over after school and shoot some hoops?" asks DJ with pure excitement.

"Absolutely!" says Lil Mar, as they all start to make their way to class.

"Mrs. Adams will be giving us back our math tests today and I hope I did very well on it. I studied really hard for this test!" says Lucia.

"ME TOO!" Elec and DJ shout in unison.

"Hey, Lil Mar, didn't you get the best grade in class on the last math test?" asks Elec.

"Yep, I got a 100% and the bonus question." Lil Mar replies.

"Wow," the others gasp with envy as they enter Mrs. Adams' classroom. Lil Mar isn't worried, as he always gets good grades on his school work.

Later that afternoon, right before the school dismissal bell, the moment has finally arrived for Mrs. Adams to pass out the results for the, 'Big Math Test!' Some students were a little nervous about the test, but Lil Mar was super excited to receive his results. Again, he always gets great grades in class.

Mrs. Adams informs all of the students that when she calls their name, they can come up and get their test results before being dismissed for their buses. Mrs. Adams calls a few names and hands them their test results, with a smile on her face and a 'good job' as students exit the class.

"Elec," Mrs. Adams calls. When Elec receives his test, a big smile comes across his face, and a very enthusiastic, "YES!" as he raises both hands high in the air then exits the classroom.

"Lucia...DJ" calls Mrs. Adams with a pleasant smile on her face.

"YAY!" shouts Lucia.

"NICE!" shouts DJ, as they both turn around and give each other high fives.

Lil Mar sits patiently, waiting for his name to be called as the rest of the class receives their test results.

Last but not least, Mrs. Adams calls his name, "Lil Mar".

Lil Mar hops out of his seat and makes his way up to get his test with a big smile on his face. As he approaches Mrs. Adams, he notices the smile his teacher had given all of the other students, was not quite the same.

"Lil Mar," says Mrs. Adams, slowly, as the smile on her face changes to a look of concern.

"Yes…Mrs. Adams", he almost reluctantly replies.

"After grading your work, I'm going to go out on a limb and assume that you did not study for this math test," says Mrs. Adams.

Just then a troubled look came across Lil Mar's face. She hands Lil Mar his test results and there are so many red marks on his paper it looks like his paper is bleeding and needs first aid! On the top of his paper, in big, bold, red ink, it has the letter 'F' with a sad frown face right next to it.

"Did you study like the rest of the class?" his teacher asks. "Well…ummm…not really," Lil Mar replies.

He immediately starts thinking how he has been consumed with playing a lot of basketball lately, as well as spending hours playing the hottest new video game, 'Force Light'.

"Well, unfortunately I'm going to need your mother to sign this test and you can return it back to me by the end of the week" she says.

A look of horror flashes across Lil Mar's face as he knows that his mother will not be happy about his test results.

"Okay Mrs. Adams" he replies as he buries his chin into his chest while his face flushes with embarrassment.

The fear of showing this paper to his mother is the only thing on his mind.

Mrs. Adams gently places her hand on Lil Mar's chin and slowly lifts his head and she says, "No need to put your head down, Lil Mar! When you study and apply yourself, there is nothing in this world that you cannot do. There will be a written exam next week on, 'Future Career Occupations'. If you balance your studies and play, you will have no problem getting a high score on the next test."

"Okay...Thank You," he replies as he slowly walks out of Mrs. Adams classroom to catch his bus.

Lil Mar is absolutely devastated! His mind is only consumed with his low-test score and how in the world he is going to break the horrible news to his mother. He heads to his bus. Completely ashamed by his test result, he folds up the test and hides it in a small compartment of his book bag.

The bus is almost full as he makes his way to the very last seat so he can be all alone. Still sad about his paper, he puts his hands over his face as the bus travels along. Stop after stop, other students exit the bus. The bus is now empty.

Lil Mar is still at the back of the bus with his face buried in his hands.

The bus driver yells out, "Last stop!"

Lil Mar finally removes his hands from his face and makes his way to the front of the bus.

"Thank you," says Lil Mar to the bus driver as he exits the bus.

"You're welcome," the bus driver replies, as Lil Mar steps off the school bus.

As the bus pulls away, Lil Mar notices that the bus number on the back of the bus is #88 and not his normal bus, #22. Nothing in the neighborhood looks familiar to him.

"OH NO! I GOT ON THE WRONG BUS! I do not know how to get home from here!" He cries.

Lil Mar was so devastated about his math test that he didn't realize that he had ridden home on the wrong bus.

He decides to walk a few blocks to see if he could possibly recognize anything, or anyone, that would help him find his way home. After walking several blocks in this unfamiliar neighborhood, he realizes that he is lost.

"What am I going to do now?" he says to himself as his eyes started to slightly fill with tears.

Lil Mar's day went from bad, because of his poor test, to worse, because now he is lost. He decides to sit on the curb of the street until he can come up with a plan to find his way home.

Still sad about his test, on top of being lost, he puts his face back in his hands as he tries to figure out his plan to make it home.

As he sits on the curb, of a street unknown to him, he hears a voice "Hey Bud...Are you Okay?"

Lil Mar removes his face from his hands and looks up.

It's a police officer, sitting in a police cruiser. He has seen police officers before in his neighborhood and other places, but has never actually talked to an officer in person.

"Ummm...Hi, Officer...Ummm...I'm kind of lost and do not know my way home from here." says Lil Mar nervously.

"Lost?" the officer replies. "No worries, Bud, I can help you get home," as he opens the door of his police cruiser. He steps out and approaches Lil Mar.

As the officer approaches Lil Mar, he notices that Lil Mar appeares to be sad and a little more afraid with every step he takes closer towards him.

All of a sudden, the officer is standing directly in front of Lil Mar. Now, Lil Mar is starting to feel goosebumps on his arms as the officer stands before him. The officer is wearing a dark blue uniform, with a very shiny badge, and a lot of gadgets strapped around his waist.

"Hi, I'm Officer Sharpe...What's your name?" he says, with a big smile on his face.

Lil Mar is still a little unsure about Officer Sharpe. Kids and adults in his neighborhood sometimes talk bad about the police, and a lot of them are afraid of the officers.

This particular police officer seems especially kind, and like he genuinely wants to help him out.

"My name is Lil Mar," he replies.

Officer Sharpe reaches out his fist to give Lil Mar a fist bump. "It's a pleasure to meet you!" says Officer Sharpe.

"It's a pleasure to meet you too, Officer Sharpe!" he replies, as he reaches out his arm to fist bump Officer Sharpe back.

"Hop in my cruiser and I'll get you home," says Officer Sharpe.

Instantly, a smile comes across Lil Mar's face as he stands up from the curb and makes his way over to the police cruiser. A sense of purpose and wonder washes over him.

"I have never been in a police cruiser or even spoken to a real officer before," says Lil Mar.

"Oh, wow!" Officer Sharpe replies. "Never?" he asks excitedly. "No, Never, Sir!" Lil Mar replies.

"Maybe I can show you how to operate some of the controls in my cruiser on the way to your house. If that's okay with you?" asks Officer Sharpe.

Intsantly, Lil Mar's smile becomes even bigger than before; hearing he could operate the controls of Officer Sharpe's cruiser. Lil Mar anxiously hops in the police car and fastens his seat belt. "What's your address Lil Mar?" asks Officer Sharpe.

"1231 7th Avenue" he replies.

"Wow, I used to live in that neighborhood when I was about your age!" Officer Sharpe says.

"You were once my age?" asks Lil Mar, in total shock and disbelief.

"It was a long time ago, but yes, I was your age once," Officer Sharpe says as he starts to laugh, which also makes Lil Mar laugh.

Officer Sharpe starts his police car and they head to Lil Mar's house.

On the way to Lil Mar's house, Officer Sharpe explains the function of all of the buttons in his police cruiser and allows Lil Mar to operate the spotlight, as well as talk on the megaphone.

Officer Sharpe also gives Lil Mar a few snacks and a bottle juice from the backseat of his police cruiser. He explains to Lil Mar he keeps these in his police cruiser to give to kids in the community while he is on duty.

Lil Mar is so excited, he totally forgets about the bad day he has had.

"So, how did you end up so far away from your neighborhood, Lil Mar?" asks Officer Sharpe.

At that moment, the excitement of all of the fancy controls in Officer Sharpe's cruiser comes to an end, as Lil Mar was instantly reminded of the awful day he had at school.

"Well, Officer Sharpe," he slowly replies, "I always get really good grades in school, and today, I received a very bad grade on my math test, and it has me really down."

"I see," says Officer Sharpe.

"I also have to show my test to my mom, and I know she will not be happy about my bad grade," he adds.

"Lil Mar, did you study for your test?" asks Officer Sharpe.

"Well...Ummm...no I didn't," Lil Mar replies as he lowers his head.

"Why not?" asks Officer Sharpe.

"Well, I've been spending a lot of time lately working on my basketball game and I've also been spending a lot of time playing my new game called, 'Force Light'," Lil Mar replies.

"'Force Light'...I love playing that game!" says Officer Sharpe. "I play it all of the time."

"Officer Sharpe, you play 'Force Light'?" Lil Mar asks surpried.

"Ha-ha, of course I do, Lil Mar…after I take care of all of my responsibilities, that is," says Officer Sharpe.

Lil Mar pauses for a moment, as he looks down at the ground. He slowly lifts his head with a confused look on his face

"When do you have time to play, 'Force Light' and do your job as a police officer?" he asks.

Officer Sharpe chuckles a little, "It's called balance, young man!"

Lil Mar, still with a confused look on his face replies, "Balance?" He recalls Mrs. Adams mentioning this word to him after he received his poor test grade.

"Yes, Lil Mar, balance is making sure that I get all of my work done before I am able to do all of the fun things I like. I call it 'All Work…Before Play'!"

Lil Mar pauses as he thinks about what Officer Sharpe has said for a couple of seconds.

"Oh…I get it!" Lil Mar says with an excited look on his face. "If I would have taken time and studied before I played basketball and 'Force Light', I would have had a better grade on my test!" says Lil Mar as if he had just had the biggest revelation ever.

"Yep, Lil Mar, you are absolutely correct!" says Officer Sharpe.

"From here on out, I am going to have more balance in getting my studies done before I play basketball and 'Force Light', so I do not get a bad grade on my next test, or any other test in the future," says Lil Mar.

"Sounds like a plan of a champion, if you ask me. When is your next test?" asks Officer Sharpe.

"It's next week, and the subject is on, 'Future Career Occupations'. I have no idea what I want to be when I grow up," Lil Mar replies.

"Well, I am sure that you will come up with something, and whatever it is, I am sure that you will be great at anything you choose," says Officer Sharpe as Lil Mar continues to play with all of the illuminated buttons in his police cruiser.

Finally, Officer Sharpe and Lil Mar arrive at his home, 1231 7th Avenue.

"Is this your house?" asks Officer Sharpe. "Yes sir!" replies Lil Mar.

Officer Sharpe pulls his cruiser into the middle of the driveway and puts the cruiser to park. They both take off their seatbelts and get out of the police cruiser and start to head to the front door of Lil Mar's home.

Before Officer Sharpe and Lil Mar can get to the front steps of his home, the front door hastily opens, and it is Lil Mar's mom.

"Oh my, is everything okay?" asks Lil Mar's mom.

"Yes, Mom, everything is fine. This is Officer Sharpe and he was just bringing me home," Lil Mar replies.

"Bringing you home?" his mother asks with a hint of shock in her voice.

"Well...I kind of... got on the wrong bus today after school... and ended up...a little lost," says Lil Mar hesitantly.

"Oh...My!" his mother replies, still a little shocked from what she has just heard.

"Yes, but I am okay because Officer Sharpe stopped and checked on me, then brought me home! He even let me operate the buttons in his police cruiser!" he replies to his mother with pure excitement in his voice.

"Oh...my...thank you Officer Sharpe for bringing Lil Mar home!" says his mother.

"No problem at all, ma'am, just doing my job to make sure everyone in the community is safe!" says Officer Sharpe.

Lil Mar's mom holds her arms wide open, while Lil Mar steps toward his mother, and she gives him a super big hug.

"I love you, Lil Mar, and I am so glad that you are home safe," says his mother.

"I love you, too, Mom!" he replies, as Officer Sharpe stood there with a big smile on his face.

"Well, I guess I will leave and head back to work now. Take care, ma'am…take care Lil Mar and if you ever need anything, feel free to give me a call," says Officer Sharpe, as he hands Lil Mar a 'Cop Card' with a picture of him on the front and information about him on the back.

"WHOOOOOAAAA!" says Lil Mar, as Officer Sharpe smiles and makes his way back toward his police car.

"WAIT!!!" yells Lil Mar as Officer Sharpe walks away.

Officer Sharpe turns around to see Lil Mar in a full sprint heading toward him. His arms are open wide and he gives Officer Sharpe a gigantic hug.

"Thank you, Officer Sharpe, for bringing me home safely and letting me operate the controls in your police cruiser, too!" says Lil Mar.

At that moment, Lil Mar realizes that all of the bad things he heard about police officers couldn't be true. Officer Sharpe hugs Lil Mar back then kneels down on one knee to get eye to eye with Lil Mar.

"No problem at all, Lil Mar! It is my job to serve and protect, for any and every person in the community!" says Officer Sharpe, before giving Lil Mar another big hug. He then gets into his police criuser and drives away.

Officer Sharpe pulls his police cruiser out of Lil Mar's driveway, honks his air horn twice, and waves while pulling out.

Lil Mar waves back at Officer Sharpe as he travels down the street. He continues to wave until he can no longer see Officer Sharpe's police cruiser.

Lil Mar turns around, "MOM...THAT WAS SO COOL! I'VE NEVER MET A POLICE OFFICER BEFORE...AND I'VE NEV- ER SAT IN A POLICE CRUISER BEFORE, EITHER!" shouts Lil Mar, to his mother.

"I bet that was exciting," says Lil Mar's mom. "But Lil Mar... My concern is how in the world, did you end up on the wrong bus?" she asks with a puzzling look.

Lil Mar's shoulders instantly drop, his head sinks, and his heart feels like it is about jump out of his chest. He slowly removes his book bag from his shoulders, reaches inside the small compartment and removes a folded-up paper.

"Well, Mom, I kind of have something to show you," says Lil Mar, as he slowly hands his mom the folded-up paper. His Mom unfolds the paper, takes a glance at it.

"WHOA!" his mom exclaims, as her eyes go back and forth in disbelief from Lil Mar to the red ink-covered paper.

Lil Mar places his hands behind his back, twiddles his thumbs, while shamefully lowering his head.

"Lil Mar, this is definitely not one your better test grades and, honestly...I cannot really say that I am surprised at this test score," says his mom.

Lil Mar's lower jaw instantly drops. His eyes are as big as two silver dollars and his eyebrows have almost jumped completely off of his face.

"You are not surprised?" Lil Mar asks shocked "Well...not really, son," his mom replies.

Lil Mar was very unsure of how to respond to his mother, and he was almost ashamed to ask her why. Lil Mar stands silently in front of his mother as he tries to gather himself and process his mother's comment.

"Son, for the last week, I've watched you play basketball and, 'Force Light' from the moment you arrive home from school, all the way up until your bedtime. I never once witnessed you study... for one second," says his mom.

Lil Mar stands there reflecting on the accuracy of his mother's statement.

"In life, Son, what you put in to something, is what you will get out of it. Unfortunately, you did not put enough effort into your studies, therefore you received this mistake-ridden test in return," says his mom, as she continues to look at his test.

"Somewhere along the way Lil Mar, you...,"

However, before his mother could complete her sentence, Lil Mar interupts and finishes her sentence for her, by saying, "I know Mom...I lost my focus," as he raises both of his hands, while shrugging his shoulders.

He utters the same exact words he heard from Mrs. Adams and Officer Sharpe. "Lil Mar, you took the words right out of my mouth," his mother replies, as a grin appears on her face.

Lil Mar's mom reaches out towards him and grabs his hand, then pulls him in close for the biggest 'Mommy' hug ever.

"Use this as a learning experience, Son," says his mother. "I need you to develop a blueprint on how to maintain and balance your priorities, to avoid grades like this in the future."

Lil Mar looks up and smiles at his mother and says, "Absolutely!"

Lil Mar is starting to feel better now that he has overcome the obstacle of showing his mom the disappointing test. He is also very determined to develop a plan to balance his school work and all of the fun things that he loves to do.

He has the entire weekend to come up with a strategic blueprint to get himself back on track and to start on his big paper for next week on, 'Future Career Occupations'.

Lil Mar reaches into his book bag, and pulls out two blank sheets of paper. He sits at the kitchen table while his mom prepares dinner. Before he starts to write on the paper, he reflects on his day. Lil Mar thought about how amazing it was to sit inside of a police cruiser, work all of the controls, and how awesome it was to meet an actual police officer.

"Officer Sharpe was so cool, and he brought me home after I was lost!" says Lil Mar to himself.

He thought about what Mrs. Adams and Officer Sharpe said about the importance of balancing school, work, and play. He began to realize that this will be important for his future success. He picks up his pencil and begins to write headings at the top of each paper.

At the top of the first paper, he writes 'Balance Schedule'. Lil Mar makes a weekly chart on how much time he would spend doing his homework, shooting hoops, hanging with friends and how much time he will spend playing, 'Force Light'. At the bottom of the page, he wrote in big, bold letters something Mrs. Adams told him earlier that day, 'THERE IS NOTHING IN THIS WORLD I CANNOT DO!'

At the top of the second paper, he writes, 'Thank You Officer Sharpe'. Underneath, Lil Mar draws a picture of him and Officer Sharpe sitting in a police cruiser with big smiles on their faces.

"Lil Mar, go wash your hands, it is time for dinner," his mother calls out, as she finishes preparing dinner.

"Okay, Mom," he replies, as he walks over to his mother to show her the, 'Balance Schedule' and thank you note. His mother looks at both papers, with a smile ear to ear, and says "Very impressive, Son!"

Lil Mar is extremely proud of his, 'Balance Schedule' and thank you note. He couldn't wait to start utilizing his new, 'Balance Schedule' this weekend and he was even more excited about giving Officer Sharpe his thank you letter.

Soon after Lil Mar finishes that thought, a look of concern comes across his face and he says, "How am I going to get this thank you note to Officer Sharpe?"

THE END

LaMar Sharpe is an eighteen year veteran with the Canton City Police Department. Sharpe is currently assigned to the Community Involvement Unit (CIU), where his focus is on improving and building stronger communities. He is also the founder and president of the nonprofit organization, Be a Better Me Foundation.

Sharpe has won numerous community awards, as well as State of Ohio awards for his ongoing commitment to help build a better future for our youth. Sharpe has a social media following that he uses to help promote positive change. Sharpe also started his own book publishing company named Sharpe Vision; to help promote literacy and allow youth to write and publish their own books at no cost.

In his limited free time, he is an assistant varsity football coach a McKinley Senior High School. Sharpe is married to Deidra and together they have a blended family of nine amazing kids, Imari, Xzavier, Armani, Trysten, Cameron, Alexa, Landon, La- Mar Jr. and Desmond. He also has three beautiful grandchildren, London, Aurora and Elijah.

Grayson Switzer is an American artist. Known on Instagram as 'grayson.tea'. Grayson found his passion for art through his father. The two would often watch Saturday morning cartoons or make each other crazy characters on a napkin. Grayson loves painting and using chalk pastels to make elaborate portraits in his free time. As of late, Grayson has been focused on digital art and animation. He aspires to work in the animation field.

MEET THE PEOPLE BEHIND
THE CHARACTERS

Mrs. Adams

Kara Adams is a 3rd grade teacher in the Canton City School District in Canton, Ohio, and is dedicated to the success and growth of each one of her students. She is not only passionate about shaping the lives of her young pupils, but makes each day fun and exciting.

DJ

DJ is an outstanding 5th grade student in the Canton City School District in Canton Ohio. He is super athletic and very outgoing. DJ and Officer Sharpe met each other while he was patrolling in his neighborhood many years ago. They are really great buddies to this day.

Elec

Elec is a world renowned musical talent and has traveled across the country performing in front of hundreds and thousands of people. He is a former musician in the hit Broadway show 'Stomp' and is currently traveling the world with the music group 'Pieces of A Dream'. Elec is also known for his must-see antibullying shows that he performs at school everywhere.

Lucia

Lucia is a very gifted and talented young lady that attends school in the Plain Local School District in Canton, Ohio. The author has known Lucia since she was a baby and he often visits her at school and have lunch with her, while on duty.

Lil Mar

Lil Mars character is inspired by the authors oldest grandson.

Lil Mar's Mom

The character of Mom is inspired by the author's mother.

Made in the USA
Columbia, SC
06 March 2021

33728011R00031